Contents

For Kelly, Jade and Billy

1 Football Practice

Shazia and Paula were in different classes. They never noticed each other until one playtime when Shazia was kicking a plastic football around on the netball court. Paula joined in. Then Mrs Finch told them that they were being too rough, and the little ones might get knocked over, and why didn't they do some proper netball practice. After that they were friends.

"You know I had to work in the shop all Sunday?" said Shazia one morning. They were in the cloakroom, admiring her new football. It was hand-stitched leather, blue and white. "My cousin was away in London. Well, my uncle went to the warehouse yesterday and got a load of these balls, and my father said I could have one for working on Sunday. It's real leather, see. My uncle wanted me to have a girl sort of present, but I chose this."

Paula felt the ball in her hand. It was heavy. She had only played with a plastic ball before, but in games lessons the boys had started to use leather footballs. Plastic ones were just for the infants. She bounced it on the cloakroom floor. It smacked down on the concrete, and didn't leap up again the way the plastic ones did. Shazia's name was written on the ball in ink.

"I wish you had let me write the name on for you," said Paula. "I'd have done it really small and neat along the edge of one of the white patches here. It doesn't look so brand-new, with your scrawly writing all across it."

Shazia glanced at the ball. "I would have asked you to do it if I'd thought," she said. "But who cares? I only wanted the ball for kicking, not to put up on the shelf for an ornament. Come on, we haven't got long. Let's try it out."

They ran outside.

There were three parts to the playground. There was a grassy patch, with logs for climbing, where the infants mostly played if it was dry enough. There was the netball pitch, where the little ones played if the grass was too muddy, and where the girls walked about or played games; or they could practise shooting netballs through the metal rings on the wall.

Then there was the football pitch, which was the biggest space, but only the older boys played there. Usually there were several games being played at once, and the boys made different goals with piles of jackets. Some of the boys, like Richard from

Paula's class, were useless at football, but they still raced up and down, using up all the space.

If anyone tried to set up a different game on the football pitch, like hopscotch or skipping, the boys would get a teacher to come and tell them to move. They were allowed to have the football pitch just for their games. Of course, you could do some useful training up against the wall.

"I don't see why we shouldn't play on the proper football pitch," said Paula. "After all, we are using a proper football."

Both of the real goals were being used, so they practised some heading, and then fast dribbling up and down the edge of the pitch. Mr Crendon had been showing the boys a way of kicking the ball with different sides of your feet, running along the lines marked on the tarmac.

"We'll need to do leg-strengthening exercises," said Shazia. She tapped the ball gently across to Paula.

"Got a new ball?" Some of the boys had noticed them. "Borrowed it off your brother, did you? Can I have a go?"

"I don't have any brothers," said Shazia. "It's

my ball. It's a real leather one. We'll play with you
if you like.''

Anthony kicked the ball away from under
Paula's foot and dashed off with it across the pitch.
Paula and Shazia raced after him. As soon as they
came close to him, he passed to Montaz. It was like
being a team of two against thirty or forty boys.
Paula and Shazia couldn't get near the ball.

Paula felt angry. She chased after the ball until the breath hurt her chest and her legs ached. She wouldn't stop and let the boys steal the ball, but she knew there was no chance of getting it back, just her and Shazia.

But Shazia didn't seem to mind. She was behaving as though this was the game she had planned. She watched to see which way the ball would go next and, all of a sudden, when one of the boys was too slow, she had it on the end of her toe. Paula would have picked it up and walked away with it then, to stop them playing, but Shazia just kicked it, a great kick that sent it nowhere in particular, way above the boys' heads. Then she turned round and grinned at Paula. Sometimes Paula did not understand Shazia.

Mrs Finch blew the whistle to line up and go indoors. The boys disappeared from the football pitch, but before they went, one of them gave the ball a last long kick, so that it flew to the very far corner of the playground. Shazia had to go and fetch it, and she was the last person to get in line. Mrs Finch frowned at her.

"We'll make sure we play on our own next

time," Paula said to Shazia. "Those boys don't play fair. If we keep on practising, we'll be better than them, and maybe Mr Crendon will pick us for the team. He said he would be picking the team soon."

But at dinner-time the boys wanted to use Shazia's ball again.

"You're not having it if you don't let us play properly," said Paula. "We want to get in some practice. It's not fair with all of you against the two of us."

"Let us be in one of your teams," said Shazia.

"I'm not having them in my team," said Anthony. They all looked at the new football.

"They can be in my team," said Montaz, "if we can count the two of them as one person. I know – they can both be in goal."

The boys looked at Paula and Shazia, trying to work out whether they should count as one person or two. Then, as no-one else wanted to hang around in goal getting cold, they agreed to the arrangement and ran away to kick off.

"Pigs," said Paula. "Saying we're only half as good as them. Let's show them. We'll take it in turns to be in goal, each time they come up this end."

The first shot at goal was an easy one to save. Paula only had to tap it out with her foot, then she gave it a good long kick back to mid-field. She stood to one side to give Shazia her turn. Anthony came racing down the pitch and passed to Brendan, who kicked it in with a bit of a spin on it, so that it curved right into the corner. Shazia jumped up and punched it out just in time. It was a good save, but no-one cheered, the way they would have if a boy had made it.

After that the ball was mostly down the other end of the pitch, until just before the end of break, when there were three more shots at goal. Shazia and Paula managed to keep them all out, taking turns.

When the whistle blew, Montaz kicked the ball back to Shazia.

"Not bad goalkeeping, eh?" said Shazia.

"Well, it's easy enough when there's two of you," he answered.

Lining up to go indoors, Paula noticed Jackie pushing Lucy in the buggy across the playground. One afternoon a week, the school canteen was used for a toy library and people brought their little children to borrow toys to take home. Jackie was always there as soon as it opened.

Paula nudged Shazia and pointed at Jackie.

"That your mum?" Shazia asked, screwing up her eyes.

"Yes," said Paula. "But she's not my mum. Look at Lucy's head!"

Shazia looked. Lucy's head looked spiky. There were coloured things sticking out of it.

"They aren't clothes pegs, are they?"

"They are," said Paula gloomily. "Loads of them. Every day she has to have one more than the day before. She's up to eleven of them now. I had to take her down to the supermarket last night to meet Jackie, and people were pointing to her and saying, 'Look at the poor little thing, she's got glasses *and* clothes-pegs in her hair!'"

"I'm surprised that your mum lets her go out like that," said Shazia. "She always dresses her up so nicely."

"Oh, she says you have to let little children express themselves," said Paula. "It means Lucy can paint her face green if she likes, or spread marmite all over the kitchen table. I'd like to see what Jackie would say if I started expressing myself. I know where I would spread the marmite."

"What do they want to come to the toy library for, anyway?" asked Shazia. "There's always loads of toys at your place. Lucy's room is like a toy-shop, isn't it?"

"Jackie chooses puzzles and things," said Paula. "She makes Lucy do them every day, harder and harder ones. She's trying to train Lucy to be a super-brain."

"She should send her to help in our shop," said Shazia. "That soon makes you brainy, working out all the change."

Shazia's class filed indoors, leaving Paula outside. She watched Jackie park the buggy and she knew that as Lucy climbed up the steps to the canteen Jackie was counting, "One step, two steps, three steps . . ." because she never let a chance go by of teaching Lucy something.

2   Football Theory

Shazia came back to Paula's flat after school to do
her homework. If she went straight home, then her
big sister would disappear, and Shazia would be
stuck looking after the shop. It was hard to do
homework and look after the till as well, and there
was no space to spread out the books.

"Hello, Shazia," said Jackie. "Say hello to
Shazia, Lucy."

"Hello, Lucy," said Shazia. "Did you get some
nice puzzles from the toy library? We saw you in
the playground."

"I got quite an interesting one with dinosaurs,"
said Lucy. The clothes-pegs on her head clattered
against each other as she talked. "Look, it's an

iguanodon. I'm on to sixteen-piece puzzles now. Puzzles with twelve pieces are too easy for me."

Shazia liked listening to Lucy talking. She was so careful to use all the right words, and they sounded funny coming from such a small person. Shazia laughed at her sometimes, but Lucy didn't seem to notice.

Paula fetched a drink for herself and Shazia, and took them into her room.

"Come on, Shazia," she called out impatiently. "Come and tell me what this maths is all about. I never understood any of it."

Jackie was busy teaching Lucy to read. Shazia waited to see how good she was at it. Jackie showed Lucy a little card with a word on it.

"Ruh—ah—buh—buh—ih—tuh," said Lucy. "Rabbit!"

"Good girl!" said Jackie, and showed her another card.

"Your little sister is good at reading," Shazia told Paula. "Most kids can't read until they go to school, you know."

"She's only my half-sister," said Paula. "And anybody would be brilliant if they had a full-time teacher teaching them things from when they woke up in the morning to when they went to bed at night."

Paula was tired of listening to Jackie trying to make Lucy clever. Long ago, before Jackie came to live with them, it had been much quieter. Dad and Paula used to watch television or play cards together, and they could eat chips every night without being told that it was unhealthy.

Now everyone had to eat proper dinners with vegetables, and on top of that they had to hear Lucy do her reading, or say her nursery rhymes. Jackie had even started taking Lucy to violin lessons, and they had to listen to her playing her scratchy little violin. The only good thing about the violin lessons was that Jackie had to go out to work at the supermarket three evenings a week to pay for them.

After they had done their homework, Paula and Shazia looked at Paula's football book. Dad had got it from a mate at work.

"It tells you different ways of training," said Paula. "There's a section on each position in the field, and a section on the different skills. Then at the back here it has a list of all the great footballers that there's ever been."

"Maybe we'll be in all the books one day," said Shazia.

"You know we can't, don't you?" said Paula. "My dad says there's rules that stop girls playing in real matches."

"Ah, never mind," said Shazia. "There's nothing to stop us playing in school matches, and then when they see how brilliant we are, maybe they'll decide to change the rules. The big teams send scouts around to watch the school matches to spot young talent."

Lucy opened the bedroom door and came in.

"You're not doing homework, are you?" she said suspiciously.

"We've finished it," said Paula. "Anyway, you aren't doing your reading, are you?"

"I've read all my words," said Lucy. "Mummy said I could play, actually."

"Well, we're not playing, actually," said Paula.
"We're reading. So just be quiet."

Lucy leant over her shoulder and looked at the
football book. It was open at a photograph of
Kenny Dalgliesh chipping the ball in a match
against Manchester City.

"I could do that," said Lucy. "Easy." She
swung her foot at the waste-paper bin. Shazia
snatched it out of the way just in time.

"Lucy!" called Jackie. "Let's play number
dominoes!" She came and looked into the
bedroom.

"There's no need for you to be teaching Lucy
about football, Paula," said Jackie. "One tomboy
in the family is enough."

"It keeps you fit," said Shazia in her quiet, serious voice. "It gets oxygen to the brain. And it develops your co-ordination as well. Does Lucy have any physical education at the moment?"

She was joking, but Jackie looked thoughtful.

"I did hear about a toddlers' gymnastics class," she said. "I wonder if I should take her along?"

She took Lucy to play dominoes.

"Does she teach her science and history and all that?" Shazia asked.

"I wish she'd teach her geography," said Paula. "They could both go and get lost in the Southern hemisphere."

3   Proper Boots

At break the next day, Mr Crendon came out into the playground with his cup of coffee. He stood in his grey tracksuit watching the game of football that was going on. P.E. was one of the subjects that he taught. He taught other subjects as well, but he liked to look like an athlete all the time. The only time that he wore ordinary teachers' clothes was when it was his turn to do assembly.

This time Paula and Shazia were in different teams. Although Anthony and Montaz wouldn't admit that they were good, they had noticed that Shazia and Paula would be useful players. As soon as Montaz picked Paula for his team, Anthony picked Shazia for his.

"When are you choosing the school team, sir?" Paula asked Mr Crendon, while the ball was down the other end.

"Oh, sometime this week," said Mr Crendon. He jigged from foot to foot, swinging his arms as though he was running, and turning his head in circles as though he was keeping an eye on a helicopter flying round overhead. He was always exercising. "Why do you ask?"

Paula wondered whether he was joking or not. Perhaps he really didn't know that she and Shazia

played football. Mr Crendon had a bushy beard that he hid behind, so that you couldn't see the shape of his mouth, and he spoke in a flat voice which never went up or down, or louder or softer. He didn't need to have different moods, like ordinary people, because his two moods could carry on at the same time: feeling pleased with himself, and impatient with other people.

"Just hoping, sir," said Paula. "Shazia and I have been doing a lot of training."

Mr Crendon nodded and turned away from her. He was watching as Shazia took control of the ball and then passed it to Brendan.

Before break was over, Mr Crendon took out his whistle and blew it. It hung on a cord round his neck, and he kept it in his mouth.

"Not bad play," he said with his teeth shut, as the players gathered round him. Then he spat the whistle out onto his chest. "Before I pick the team, I'm going to call a training session after school. Any of you can come, but make sure you have proper boots. We're going to take this seriously."

"The girls won't be in it, will they, sir?" Richard asked. He was afraid that he was not likely to be

picked for the team. His chances would be better if
Paula and Shazia were out of the way.

Mr Crendon looked at Paula and Shazia. There
was no way of deciding whether it was a friendly
look or not.

"Let's see what you can do," he said. He took
the ball from Montaz and headed it onto the pitch.
Then he ran out after it.

"Come on," he called. "Tackle me, Paula.
Shazia, get over there ready for a pass."

He seemed to be more interested in showing off
his own skill than finding out about theirs. But
when the bell rang he said, "Not bad for girls. You

can come along if you want. Thursday, straight after school. But don't forget, proper boots. We're not having special rules for girls."

"Well, that's the first step," said Shazia. "I thought he might not even let us come to the training session."

"But it's not fair," said Paula. "The boys didn't have to prove how good they were. Any of them could come along, even the really hopeless ones like Richard Tackley. And where am I going to get boots from? I don't know why I bothered even thinking about the school team."

"I'll ask my uncle," said Shazia. "You know he can sometimes get things cheaper than in the shops. He doesn't really like me to play football, but he doesn't try to stop me. He just says that I'll grow out of it."

"I haven't got any money at all," said Paula, "even if he did get them cheap. I lose ten pence of my pocket money every time I forget to put the empty milk bottles out, or leave a light on when I'm not in the room, or don't clean round the bath, or forget to put the lid on the tooth-paste – I shan't be getting any pocket money until about June."

"Jackie isn't half strict," said Shazia. "I don't get any pocket money, but I do get a present if I do extra work in the shop. Maybe you could earn some money."

Paula thought for a while, but the idea did not cheer her up.

"It's no good," she said. "If you try to get money off strangers, they say you're too young and want to see your licence, and if you try to get it off the teachers, they expect it to be for charity. The other kids wouldn't pay me for anything anyway."

"What about borrowing some boots?" suggested Shazia. "From someone who doesn't want to be in the team? Not everyone wants to give up their free time and go to training sessions after school."

"Someone like that wouldn't have boots anyway," said Paula. "It's no good."

She felt angry with Mr Crendon, but it was no use trying to argue with him. She would have to give up the idea of the football team. She was still cross when she got home.

She was hardly inside the front door when Lucy said in a knowing voice, "I can tell you are feeling grumpy, Paula."

"Oh, shut up," said Paula, and dropped her satchel on the floor.

Jackie came out of the kitchen. She always tried to be pleasant when Paula first came in from school.

"Could you put your satchel in your room, please, Paula?" she said. "We've made some lovely rock cakes for tea, haven't we, Lucy? We read the recipe together, and then Lucy weighed out all the ingredients."

"I don't like rock cakes," said Paula. It was true. She never ate things with currants in.

"Isn't that a bit selfish, Paula?" said Jackie. "How do you think it makes your little sister feel, to hear you say that?"

Paula shut her teeth tightly together and thought, she's only half my sister, and I'm not going to make myself sick with her horrible rock cakes.

But Lucy was pleased. "We can have four each, then, Mummy, instead of three."

Paula knew that Dad didn't like rock cakes either, but when he came in he ate his four before he even got his cup of tea. He listened to Lucy reading, and heard her play 'Twinkle twinkle little star' on her violin, and admired the picture she had painted of a diplodocus.

"How about my Paula, then?" he said. "What have you been up to today?"

"Nothing much," said Paula. She didn't want to tell him about the football in front of Jackie.

"I've been finding out about that toddlers' gymnastics group," said Jackie. "It's in the Community Centre on Fridays, and it only works out at a pound a session. I thought I might take Lucy along."

Daddy shrugged his shoulders. "Sounds all right," he said, "if she enjoys that sort of thing."

They all looked down at Lucy, who was sitting

on the floor tracing round coloured shapes.

"Square," she was murmuring, "rectangle, circle, noctagon."

"Octagon, darling," said Jackie. "If it's got eight sides, it's an octagon."

"That's what I said," said Lucy, staring at Jackie as though she was very stupid. "A noctagon."

Paula wondered how many toddlers' gymnastics sessions there would be in each term. It must cost at least ten pounds every term. Suddenly, she decided to ask for the boots.

"Daddy," she said, "I need some football boots. Mr Crendon won't let me into the team unless I get some."

Daddy laughed. "And is he thinking of putting you in the team?" he asked.

"I don't know," said Paula. "He should put me in. I'm not the fastest, but I am good. I'm better than most of the boys. But he won't even consider me unless I've got boots."

"Well, we could think about it, couldn't we," said Jackie. Paula knew that she meant, "Let's wait until she forgets about it."

"I need them for Thursday," said Paula.

"But if he doesn't pick you," said Daddy, "then what? We'll have a spare pair of boots on our hands. They aren't cheap, you know."

"Well, I'll use them, won't I?" said Paula. "Shazia and me play every playtime, and in the evenings when it's not dark. Go on, Daddy."

"Quite honestly," said Jackie, "I'd rather spend the money on ballet lessons, or something you were more likely to stick at. This football is only a passing phase. I mean, you'll be into hockey and netball in a year or so."

"How long does it have to last, to be a phase that hasn't passed?" asked Paula indignantly. "I've been playing football longer than you've known me." It was the wrong thing to say, because Jackie did not like to be reminded that she had not been around as long as Paula. Daddy tried to smooth it over. He always avoided arguments, even important ones.

"That'll do, Paula," he said. "But it's true, love, she has been kicking a ball about since she could stand on both feet, and she's seen more matches than most kids her age. But I don't see why you can't play in your ordinary trainers, Paula."

"Mr Crendon just says we have to have boots, that's all," said Paula. She sat swinging her feet against the table-legs and moving the rock-cake crumbs into lines with her finger. Dad went to fetch a cloth to wipe the table. Jackie shook her head and started to open the paper at the television pages.

Just then, Lucy jumped up from the floor, scattering her shapes. She banged Paula on the arm with a pentagon.

"I'll come and watch you beating Oxford United

if you get in the team, Paula," she said. "Come on you yellows!"

"What do you know about it, you little monkey?" said Jackie, picking Lucy up and giving her a hug. "Ouch! One of your pegs went right up my nose!"

Suddenly, it was settled. Paula seemed to have lost the argument, but there was Daddy counting the money out onto the table, and Jackie was promising to meet Paula after school to buy the boots. Paula ate one of the rock cakes out of gratitude, which put all of Lucy's calculations out.

4 Away Game

Mr Crendon picked Shazia and Paula for the team.

"My dad would have killed me if I hadn't been picked," said Paula. "He didn't want to buy me these boots."

They were practising ball control in the playground.

"Mr Crendon likes to have his teams winning," said Shazia, "so he had to choose the best players, even if he didn't really want us. Haven't you seen him at assembly, when Miss Heyford asks him to read out the results? He looks as though he'd scored all the goals himself, instead of just shouting at the kids if they don't play well."

"He's so unfair, though," said Paula. "He was

talking about bringing one of us off at half-time, to give the substitute a chance. Why should it be us that comes off, and not one of the others?"

"He's just old-fashioned," said Shazia. "He doesn't think girls can be serious players. But at least he's given us a chance. I wish he'd put me further forward, though. People notice you more if you score. Even if someone is brilliant in defence, nobody notices them."

"My dad is just the same as him," Paula went on. "He thinks it's a joke, me playing football, even though it was him that taught me to play when I was little. He won't even bother coming to watch the match."

"Maybe Jackie will bring Lucy," said Shazia. "She likes giving her new experiences, doesn't she? Like when they came to the harvest service, and Lucy sang 'Combine harvester' at the top of her voice when we were supposed to be singing 'Kumbayah'—don't you remember?"

Paula was not going to be cheered up. At first she had thought that being picked for the team would be wonderful, but it still seemed that they weren't counted as real players. Mr Crendon had told them that the playing fields, where the match against the Our Blessed Lady of Brieve Middle School would be held, would have no changing facilities for girls, so Paula and Shazia had to go already changed into shorts and shirts.

"What does it matter?" asked Shazia. "If you're cold you can wear your coat over the top."

"He was threatening us as well," said Paula. "He was looking over our way when he said that he might have to rearrange the team if we didn't do well. He meant, if we don't play three times as well

as all the rest, he'll chuck us out."

Shazia shrugged her shoulders. "I suppose it's just as bad for a boy who wants to do a girls' subject, like cooking."

"No," said Paula. "They just call him a chef and pay him double."

Montaz called them over to practise with the rest of the team. Everyone was excited about the match.

"It's a bad start, an away match," said Anthony. "The other side will have loads of supporters cheering them on, and we'll be all on our own."

"Mrs Heyford said she might come and watch," said Brendan. "Anyway, it's not as though it's miles away. Most of our parents will be there, and my Uncle Perry's coming. He can shout loud. You should hear him at some of those Oxford matches. He drowns out the rest of the crowd."

"We'd better make sure all our families do come," said Montaz. "You've got loads of uncles," he said to Shazia. "Can't you get them to come and shout for us?"

"They might," said Shazia. "I don't know, though. They don't really approve. I'll ask my aunt to come. She starts work early in the morning, and she would be free by half-past four."

Paula said nothing. She had told Dad and Jackie about the match, but Dad had said, "Half-past four? Do you want to get me sacked, walking out of work early?" and Jackie had said something about Lucy having a rest after her gymnastics, and grumbled about Paula being late home from school.

Mr Crendon drove the team to the playing field in the school minibus. Shazia and Paula sat at the back. They felt a bit silly wearing their shorts and shirts already, while all the boys were in their school clothes. They wrapped their coats round their knees to keep warm. It was an old minibus and the wind whistled in through the cracks round the dented back door. Mr Crendon drove too fast and they were all jolted about on the hard seats. Everyone shouted as they swerved round a corner.

"I hope it's not far now," said Shazia, "or my aunt will never find her way here."

Mr Crendon swung the van up onto the pavement and screeched on the brakes. On the

other side of the railings were the playing fields.
The Our Blessed Lady team were already there in
their orange and white kit. They were sponsored by
the chair factory round the corner and had the
name of the firm on their backs.

"I wish we had a proper team strip," said Shazia.
"It looks a lot better than just odd shirts and
scrappy shorts."

At least Paula had the right colour shorts, blue,
just by chance, but Anthony and Brendan's shorts
were black, and Richard's were green. Paula looked

at the Our Blessed Lady team. They looked very big.

"Are they older than us?" she asked Mr Crendon as she climbed down out of the minibus. It was windy and her legs were frozen.

Mr Crendon looked at her scornfully. "If you're feeling like that already, you'd better say so now and let the substitute play," he said.

"I didn't say I was scared of them," said Paula indignantly, but Mr Crendon had walked past her to greet the teacher from the other school. It was a woman teacher, and she shook Mr Crendon's hand with a friendly smile.

"She doesn't know that he's an enemy to girls," Shazia whispered to Paula.

The boys had run to the changing rooms to get their odd shirts and shorts on. Paula and Shazia warmed up around the edge of the pitch. When the boys came out, Mr Crendon blew his whistle and gave them a talk about watching the ball and looking for people to pass to, not trying to be the star of the match but being one of a team, making spaces for the ball to be passed into, and about the pitch being bigger than they were used to so they must not wear themselves out running up and down it. Paula thought that it was quite good advice, but not the sort of advice that Mr Crendon would take himself.

"You forgot the girls, sir," Anthony called out. "Tell them the goal's that square thing down at the end of the pitch, and you're supposed to kick the ball, not pick it up and throw it."

Mr Crendon pretended not to hear. Some of the boys laughed. Paula wanted to kill Anthony, and she was wondering whether to grab him round the neck, or to kick him to death with her new football boots, when Montaz said, "Shut up, Anthony. They know more about football than you do."

Brendan said, "I'll bet you Shazia could beat you on penalties."

And Richard Tackley said, "If you upset the girls and make them drop out, then you'll have to bring the substitute on, and you know I'm nowhere near as good as them."

Paula and Shazia looked at each other, with their eyes wide open. They knew themselves that they were good, but it was the first time anyone else had said anything better than, "Not bad for girls".

The other teacher was refereeing the first half of the match. Her long hair was flying up in the wind like seaweed under water. She blew her whistle for the players to take their positions. Paula looked at the boy playing against her. He was taller than her, and he looked very smart in the orange shirt. He had a nice wide face that looked like the sun.

"Hello," he said. "Is this the first match your team has played this season?"

"Yes," said Paula. "And it's the first match I've ever played in."

"I was only a substitute last year," said the boy. "What's your name? I'm Alison."

"Are you a girl?" Paula asked in disbelief. "I thought Shazia and I were the only ones."

The girl laughed. She still looked quite like a boy.

"Have you got other girls in your team?" asked Paula. She looked round. The teachers were looking at their watches and talking. She saw that one of the players in orange had long fair plaits down her back. And there was a plump one with a fringe who must be a girl, too. It was strange that they had all looked like boys when she first glanced at them.

"There are six of us usually," said Alison. "But two of the girls are off with flu at the moment. There are some boys ill as well. We only just managed to get a team together today."

The teacher blew her whistle and, as the ball hurtled down to the far end of the pitch, Paula heard Shazia call to her. She looked over. Shazia was pointing to the side-line.

"Keep your eye on the ball!" Mr Crendon was yelling.

Paula looked over to where Shazia pointed. There were a lot of grown-ups standing on the side-line, and some of the Our Blessed Lady schoolchildren had stayed on after school to cheer on their team. Among the crowd Paula could see two of Shazia's aunts and an uncle, and three little cousins.

Paula glanced back to see whether the ball was near enough to worry about. It was still near the other goal.

She looked back at the crowd of supporters. Shazia's cousins and some other little children were screaming, "One, two, three, four, who d'you think we're shouting for, Oxford United!"

Paula saw them put their heads together to plan their next chant. Suddenly a mob of players tangled their way down the pitch as the ball came down to Paula's end. All of the Our Blessed Lady team wanted a shot at goal, and none of them wanted to pass the ball. Alison ran backwards, hoping for a pass. Paula got ready to stop the ball if it did come their way.

Mr Crendon was screaming to his team to spread out. The other teacher could not shout at her team because she was being the referee, and must not help one side more than the other. But the parents and big brothers and sisters on the side-lines were all yelling advice. Paula noticed that Brendan, who

was the goalkeeper, had come out of goal and was hopping around the mass of people, impatient to get a kick at the ball.

In the crowd nobody could see where the ball was going. It suddenly shot out and Alison was ready to take a good shot at goal. Brendan had no time to get back in goal, and it was left undefended. Quickly Paula raced for the ball and with her right foot, which was not her best one, managed to get in just before Alison and kicked it up to the other end of the pitch.

Alison had been swinging her leg ready to kick the ball, and she could not stop in time. Her foot met Paula's leg and they fell in a tangle on the muddy grass. But the ball had got clear. With all of the Our Blessed Lady team up at this end, there was no one to stop it going clear down to the other goal. Shazia passed it on to Montaz, and he was able to knock it in easily. The boy in goal made a good effort at saving it, but it all happened too quickly for him. He dived to the side, but the ball sailed in above him. Perhaps he had hit his head on the post. He leant against it looking rather giddy.

The referee blew the whistle, one-nil. Paula and

Alison stood up stickily and looked at the black mud on their shorts and legs. Paula thought she should have some bruises as well, but the mud could be covering them up. She was certainly not going to make a fuss about them, the way that Brendan would have done, rolling about on the ground and pretending that his leg was broken. As the players trotted back to their positions, the referee pointed to Paula and nodded. "Good play," she called. Paula was glad that someone had noticed, even if Mr Crendon was only interested in the ball going into the goal, and not how it had got down that end.

Suddenly Paula heard another scream from the little children on the side-line.

"One, two, three, four, which team do we want to score?"

The answer was a mixed scream, but Paula thought she could hear her own name, "Paula!" and Shazia's as well. She looked over and was amazed to see that it was Lucy standing shouting with Shazia's cousins. Paula glanced back at the pitch, then looked round again to see Jackie standing next to Shazia's aunts. She had to look twice to be sure. One of the aunts was waving her arms; perhaps they were discussing tactics. Jackie was huddled in her big quilted coat, with her hands pushed down into her pockets. She was listening and nodding.

Lucy and Shazia's cousins had linked arms, and they were stamping their feet and shouting, "Oxford United!"

"Which side do those kids think they are on?" asked Alison.

"They're supporting us," said Paula. She laughed. Lucy looked so nice, all wrapped up in her coat and mittens, with her scarf tied twice round her neck and her naughty little eyes shining out above it. "That one with the clothes-pegs in her hair, she's my little sister," Paula told Alison. "I'm planning to train her up to be a real footballer."

5   Substitute

At half-time the score was still one-nil and Mr Crendon called the team together to say the same sort of things as he had said before the game started. Paula thought he might have praised the people who had made the goal, but he was just complaining that one goal was not enough.

"It's much too easy to relax once you are in the lead," he said. "You've got to keep on pushing at them and really get them on the run. You should be able to smash them easily; they are only a bunch of girls."

Paula felt her face getting hot. How dare he say that girls were no good! She looked across at Shazia, and felt quite indignant when she saw that

Shazia was smiling calmly.

"I think there are some refreshments over by the changing rooms," said Mr Crendon. "Any questions?"

Shazia raised her hand. Mr Crendon twitched his eyebrows at her. He did not waste energy.

"Don't you think they could have smashed us quite easily in the first half," Shazia asked, "if it hadn't been for the girls in our team?"

Mr Crendon tossed his head and started walking towards the changing rooms. "This is a team game, Shazia," he said, "and if you are just looking for individual praise you had better find yourself a different sport."

"Why should he be allowed to be so mean and rude?" said Paula to Shazia. "It's disgusting. I'd like to find out what team it is he plays for on Sundays and bribe the referee to send him off after two minutes. I probably wouldn't even need to do any bribing. I expect he's so mean and unfair that he gets sent off anyway for sneakily kicking people and cheating."

"My uncle says he used to be quite a good player," said Shazia. "He used to play for the

Blackbird Rovers. I think he's a bit past it now."

Paula drank her orange squash and frowned around at everyone.

"What are you in a bad mood for now?" asked Lucy, who was standing behind her. "I thought you would be pleased because our team is winning. Did you see the goal? Wham! Right in the net! Zainum and I have been practising with our scarves rolled up in a ball, but they keep coming undone."

Paula undid her frown and smiled at Lucy.

"Well done, Paula," said Jackie. "You seem to be doing well. I've never watched a football match before. It's quite interesting."

Now that Paula was standing still, she was feeling cold. The mud had dried on her legs and felt tight and itchy.

"I'm glad you came," she said. "I didn't think we would have many people cheering us on."

"Lucy!" said Jackie. "What have you done with your scarf? There's mud all down it! Really, I knew I shouldn't have brought you. And look at your tights. Just try to keep on the dry grass. There's no need to go galloping around in the mud."

"I'm just practising what I learned at gymnastics, Mummy," said Lucy. She skipped away with Shazia's cousins, and Paula saw her trying to do a handstand and then wiping her muddy hands on her coat.

The two teachers were talking to each other. Mr Crendon waved his hand towards Shazia and Paula, and the teacher from the other school, Miss Whiteham, was nodding.

"Come here, you two," called Mr Crendon. "The Our Blessed Lady goalkeeper has had to drop out. He banged his head in the first half and Miss Whiteham is sending him home. They haven't got a substitute, so I've said that they can have one of our girls. We can bring our substitute on instead. Which one do you want, Miss Whiteham?"

"Well, thank you very much," said Miss Whiteham. "Which of you is best in goal, do you think?"

"Shazia's easily the best," said Paula. "Nearly as good in goal as on the pitch."

"Fine," said Miss Whiteham, and Shazia ran down to the goal. She must try to forget that she wanted her own team to win, and do her best to stop them scoring. She was worried that if she should let a goal in, even if she did her best, the other team might not believe that she had really tried to stop it.

The whistle blew and Paula went back to her position.

"You didn't get changed out, then," said Alison. "Is that your substitute over there, that boy with the baggy shorts?"

"Yes," said Paula. "And your teacher borrowed my friend to play in goal for you, because your goalie banged his head. It's funny to see her on the other side."

The ball came down the wing and Alison ran backwards to be ready for it. Another girl passed it to her and Alison took a kick at goal. She was too far away to have any chance, Paula thought, but she was surprised what a strong kick it was. Luckily it was too high.

"Miss Whiteham will be pleased that your teacher is refereeing," said Alison, when the ball was back down the other end. "She can scream as much as she likes now."

Suddenly the ball was crossed in from the wing. There was a shot and the ball was in the back of the net before Paula had seen what happened. The score was one-all and Mr Crendon began to look very grim.

While the action was down at the other end of the pitch, Paula glanced quickly over at the spectators. The children were watching Shazia jigging up and down in goal, but Lucy didn't seem to be standing with Shazia's cousins now. After checking that the ball was nowhere near, Paula looked round. Lucy was trying to climb up someone's legs. It was Dad! He was still in his overalls, so he must have come straight from work. If it was that late, it must be nearly time for the final whistle. Paula began to panic. She suddenly wanted to win almost as much as she had wanted to be in the team to begin with.

The ball came spinning down nearly to the goal. Paula raced for it and passed to Richard, but back it came. She felt certain that the Blessed Lady team were going to score again, but she managed to get the ball and suddenly a gap opened up down the wing. There was no one to pass to, so she took the ball down with her, keeping it close by her feet ready for the chance to pass. Then horrible Anthony yelled. He could take a shot from where he was, but Paula did not want to give him the ball.

Why should I give him the chance to score?

she thought, and slowed down.

But Shazia, bouncing about in the goal, screamed "Pass it!" As soon as she had shouted she clapped her hands over her mouth. She should not have given advice to the opposing side. But there was no time to worry about it.

Paula passed the ball. She thought Anthony would score easily, but someone tackled him. It was more of an attack than a tackle, and Anthony went over like a skittle. It was nice to see him lying in the mud, but it spoilt their chances of a goal. No, Mr Crendon had blown the whistle. It was a foul, and he was giving them a penalty. Paula looked over at Shazia. She wanted Shazia to show what a good player she was, but she wanted the goal as well.

Montaz took the penalty. Paula held her breath and would not hope either way. When Shazia saved the goal, Paula found that she was feeling very pleased. A crowd of boys were banging Shazia on the back.

"Hey, Paula!" Lucy called from the side-line. "You should have told her to let it in! Then we'd have won!"

Paula waved at her and shook her head. She made her way back down to the other end and Mr Crendon blew the whistle, but before the ball had decided which way to go next, the whistle went again for the end of the match.

"Well done," said Alison. "That was great. We are quite well matched, aren't we? We've had some terrible games before, where the other side was much too good for us, or so hopeless that it was a waste of time. But this was terrific. I hope we get to play you again."

Shazia galloped over to them.

"Well saved," said Alison. "Thanks for keeping

it to a draw."

"That was a fantastic save," said Montaz. "I didn't have a chance. And you were great, Paula. Old Crendon will have to have you both in the team for the next game, and I don't suppose he'll be so keen on substituting either of you at half-time."

Several other boys went by and shouted, "Well done." One-all was a good score for the first match of the season, and an away game as well. And Dad had arrived in time to see that the football boots had been well worth buying.

Shazia and Paula fetched their coats and stood shivering outside the changing rooms while the boys threw their shorts around inside.

"I wonder what Mr Crendon will say when he announces the result in assembly," said Shazia. "I am pleased to announce a one-all draw, achieved thanks to my super-skilful tactical substitution."

"I'm surprised he didn't demand a transfer fee," said Paula.

"A million pounds?" said Shazia.

"A tube of smarties more likely," said Paula, and Shazia chased her all the way to minibus.